The *Beautiful* Elephant

The *Beautiful* Elephant

A Script Based on a True Story of the Elephant Killings

JOSEPHINE DEBOIS

THE BEAUTIFUL ELEPHANT

This book is written to provide information and motivation to readers. Its purpose is not to render any type of psychological, legal, or professional advice of any kind. The content is the sole opinion and expression of the author, and not necessarily that of the publisher.

Printed in the United States of America.

ISBN 978-1-949746-83-9 (Paperback)
ISBN 978-1-949746-84-6 (Digital)

Lettra Press books may be ordered through booksellers or by contacting:

Lettra Press LLC
18229 E 52nd Ave.
Denver City, CO 80249
1 303 586 1431 | info@lettrapress.com
www.lettrapress.com

Dedicated to
The Royal Danish Family
in appreciation of their numerous efforts and
support for the conservation of the
wildlife of the world

Exterior: Kenya—Village at Dawn

The day is breaking. The small town with ten circular primitive huts is in a small open area in the dense forest. It is close to the border between the forest and the open savanna, reaching to the horizon. The small huts are surrounded by a primitive wooden fence to protect against wild animals. The silence of the dawn is only broken by sporadic screams of birds and wild animals.

Interior: Kenya Village—Hut at Dawn

Semi (nine); his father, Ramo (twenty-nine); and his mother, Luno (twenty-seven), all typical Africans, are sleeping on the ground close together under a simple cover. Two other families are also asleep in the hut. Semi wakes up. He looks around. He turns and pushes Ramo gently.

SEMI, *whispering in Swahili.* Can we go and watch the animals?

Ramo wakes up. He smiles at Semi while he puts his finger across his lips, signaling Semi to be silent. He takes the cover away from himself, and Semi and puts it over Luno. He takes Semi by the hand. They rise.

RAMO, *whispering in Swahili.* Come!

Semi and Ramo exit the hut.

Exterior: Kenya Village at Dawn

Semi and Ramo walk between the huts hand in hand to the exit from the small village. They push the gate carefully open and exit.

Exterior: Kenya Forest at Dawn

Ramo closes the gate to the village carefully. He takes Semi by the hand, and they run through the forest. They reach the border between the forest and the open savanna and run along the border. They reach a small lake in the open area. They go to the forest right at the border and hide behind a few bushes and fallen trees. They sit quietly and watch out over the wide savanna. In the continuing sunrise, the sky is overwhelming red with scattered clouds all around the visible horizon.

SEMI, *whispering*. Look—they are coming.

Semi and Ramo hide as they watch a herd of about twenty elephants approach the small lake. A huge elephant leads the herd. The larger elephants lead the small baby elephants to the water. The elephants all line up along the water. They drink and blow water up in the air. Semi, delighted by watching the elephants, holds Ramo tightly. He turns to Ramo, pointing at one of the baby elephants.

SEMI, *whispering*. There it is.

RAMO, *whispering*. Yes. And the mother is there.

Ramo points to a large female elephant that is taking care of its baby elephant. For a while, Semi and Ramo watch the gathering. The large elephant starts moving, and the whole herd follows it away from the lake, out to the scarce vegetation and trees on the savanna, and along the border to the forest. Semi waves goodbye to his favorite baby elephant. The elephants disappear. Semi and Ramo rise and run hand in hand back to the village. They reach the gate and look into the village.

Exterior: Kenya—Village in the Morning

The village is awake. Luno sits outside of the hut. She has lit a small fire. She is frying a few small fish. Semi and Ramo enter through the gate. Delighted, Semi runs to Luno. She embraces him.

SEMI. They were there again.

LUNO. Good. You take care of them. They take care of us. They are our souls and the souls of everything here.

Ramo comes to them, and they all sit around the small fire. They eat the fish. Life in the village becomes busy as the day breaks in full. After eating, Ramo rises. He takes Semi by the hand.

RAMO. Come—let's go to the river.

Semi and Ramo walk hand in hand to the gate. They take a few pointed wooden rods and two small fishing nets. They exit the village.

Exterior: Kenya—River at Daytime

Semi and Ramo walk through the forest. Colorful birds from the trees fly over them as they pass. Ramo points to the birds and explains the names to Semi. He takes Semi to a large tree next to the river. He points at a nest up in the tree and signals Semi to be quiet. As they stand by the tree, a bird lands in the nest and starts feeding the baby birds. Semi watches, delighted. They continue to the river's edge.

Ramo points to a row of large stones in the river. They start walking from stone to stone. In the middle of the river, they reach a large stone with space for both of them. The large stone splits the strong water stream. They lie down on the stone and fish with their nets and wooden rods.

The day passes. Semi and Ramo lie on the stone, watching the sky. The catch of several small fish is gathered in one of the nets that's kept in the water to keep the fish fresh and alive. Semi rises and sits next to Ramo, who takes his hand and holds it firmly.

They rise and again jump from stone to stone back to the river's edge. As they walk toward the village through the forest, they collect fruit from trees and bushes. Ramo shows Semi which fruit to collect and which to leave. As they search in the forest, Semi suddenly sees a baby elephant and its mother.

SEMI. Look!

They watch carefully while moving a little closer, hiding behind the bushes.

SEMI, *whispering.* Why are they not with all the others?

Ramo shakes his head. They continue to watch and get closer.

SEMI. It is hurt. It limps. Look at its leg.

A large metal nail has penetrated the skin of one of the baby elephant's front legs.

SEMI. I will help it.

Semi moves slowly toward the baby elephant. The mother elephant raises its trunk and ears.

RAMO. Stop! It is dangerous. The mother will get scared.

Semi continues to walk slowly toward the elephant. The baby elephant stands still as Semi approaches. The mother elephant moves close to the baby elephant and stands close behind. Semi raises his hand and touches the baby elephant's trunk. Semi bends down and tries to pull the metal piece out of the leg. But it is tightly stuck.

SEMI. Help me!

Ramo rises. For a moment, the mother elephant raises its trunk. Ramo approaches the baby elephant slowly. The elephants do not move. Ramo bends down and pulls the metal piece loose. In the meantime, Semi touches the baby elephant's trunk.

RAMO. Take some leaves from the bush over there.

Semi grabs a bundle of leaves. Ramo squeezes the leaves and gathers the liquid on an intact leaf. He applies it to the leg of the baby elephant and makes the liquid flow into the wound. Finally, Ramo and Semi carefully touch the leg and the trunk. The baby elephant walks back to its mother without pain. The mother elephant puts its trunk around the small elephant. It raises its trunk and makes a small trumpeting sound. The elephants walk away into the forest. Semi and Ramo gather their catch of fish. The day fades, and they walk back to the village hand in hand.

Exterior: Kenya—Village in the Evening

Semi and Ramo enter the village through the gate. Semi sees Luno. He runs to her with the net and the catch of fish. Luno embraces Semi, takes the net, and starts preparing the fish.

Semi, Ramo, and Luno sit around the fire as the last glimmers of the daylight fades. Other families sit by small fires around the courtyard. It becomes totally dark. The brilliant stars become visible. Semi leans back on Luno. She holds her arm around him while he watches the bright stars. He points at some particularly clear stars. Luno whispers the names of the stars in his ear as she points to the sky. Semi falls asleep in her arms. Ramo lifts him and carries him to the hut. They all enter. Other families leave the courtyard, leaving it empty. The moon rises. There's a silver light in the courtyard from the stars and the moon. A few screams of birds and wild animals break the silence in the night.

Transition to Dawn

Exterior: Kenya—Village at Dawn

The village is barely visible in the early dawn.

Interior: Kenya—Village Hut at Dawn

Semi lies between Ramo and Luno. He opens his eyes and listens to the screams of a few birds. He pushes Ramo, who wakes and looks at Semi's clear, expecting eyes.

RAMO, *whispering.* Okay, let's go … again.

Semi and Ramo rise and exit the hut. Luno and other families in the hut sleep fast.

Exterior: Kenya—Forest at Dawn

Again, Semi and Ramo hide and wait for the elephants by the lake. Suddenly, the trumpeting of the lead elephant breaks the silence.

SEMI, *whispering.* They come!

Semi holds Ramo's hand firmly as they watch through the branches hiding them. The herd of elephants appears. The elephants walk to the edge of the water and start drinking and bathing. The female elephants again help the youngsters. Semi's favorite elephant stands closest to them, happily enjoying the water and its mother's attention. Delighted, Semi points at the small elephant.

SEMI. Look!

Semi points to the air over the savanna. A distant rumbling sound breaks the silence. Semi looks surprised at Ramo. The sound becomes louder. The elephants stop drinking and step back from the water.

SEMI. Look!

A helicopter rapidly approaches them, flying low over the savanna. It reaches the herd with a terrible noise. The doors of the helicopter open, and four men appear in the doors, armed with heavy weapons. They shoot at the elephants.

The large lead elephant is hit. With a tremendous blow from its trumpet, though badly hurt, it moves to its female elephantto cover it from the dangers and the shooting. The gunmen continue their shooting. Elephant after elephant fall to the ground. The mother of the baby elephant is hit. While it falls, it pulls it small elephant close to fall over it and cover it. All the elephants have fallen to the ground.

The helicopter lands. The motor stops. The terrible sound of dying elephants fills the space. The gunmen carry their heavy weapons, axes, and saws, and they jump out of the helicopter. Two gunmen start sawing the tusks of the large elephant, which is still breathing, while two gunmen walk from elephant to elephant and shoot any that have survived directly in the head. They reach the female elephant covering the small elephant, which is still unhurt. One of the gunmen points his weapon toward the small elephant and shoots.

Semi screams. GUNMAN 1 (who's twenty-one with Asian traits, a scarred face, and small evil eyes) and the gang leader, JACK ZANG (who's thirty-one with Asian traits, large, robust, and strong), turn around and walk toward the hiding place of Semi and Ramo. Semi hides close to the ground under the leaves of a large branch. Ramo tries to hide. The gunman gets close to the hiding place. He sees Ramo. He points his heavy weapon toward Ramo. He shoots and hits him in the head. The headless body flies up in the air and falls in front of Semi. The blood is pumping out of the body and covers Semi. In the same moment, the tusks of the small elephant are sawed off. The gunman approaches Semi and points his gun at him.

JACK. Stop!

GUNMAN 1. He saw everything. I shoot him!

JACK. Wait! He is a child. Take him.

The gunman lowers his gun. He grasps Semi by the arm and pulls him brutally toward the helicopter. He pushes him in. A gunman in the helicopter pushes Semi down in a corner in the helicopter. Semi, frightened to death and shivering, is watching as the gunmen rapidly load the tusks of elephants in a big pile in the helicopter cargo room. The sound of the dying elephants fills the space. The last men swiftly enter the helicopter. The motor starts, and the helicopter rises.

The helicopter flies away over the savanna into the rising sun. As it flies over the savanna toward the blood-red horizon, music fills the space (Nielsen's Second Symphony, the beginning of third movement).

The music carries over.

Interior: Kenya—Helicopter at Dawn

Frightened, Semi watches from the corner in the helicopter as the landscape passes below—the village, the river, the forest. The gunmen are busily packing the tusks in large sacks. As the helicopter passes the edge of the river, Semi sees the leader elephant and the baby elephant he had helped still walking in the forest near the river. The gunmen continue packing the elephant tusks. As they grasp the tusks of Semi's favorite elephant, he cannot suppress his crying.

GUNMAN 1, *shouting*. Shut up. Are you not happy being alive? I could have blown your head off too.

He harshly throws a piece of wood at Semi. It hit the wall just next to Semi's head. Semi tries to stifle his crying. The gunmen pack their guns and remaining ammunition. The sound of the metal breaks through the music. Finally, the music fades. The men sit around in the cabin on the floor. The only sound is the motor. Some men fall asleep.

Exterior: Kenya—Landing Strip in Early Day

The helicopter lands at a small grass field close to a very primitive runway in the grass. The doors of the helicopter are swiftly opened. On the ground a group of men of African and Asian descent run to the helicopter. The sacks with tusks are quickly unloaded by the gunmen and carried by the ground crew to a small plane waiting at the runway. Jack holds Semi's arm firmly and pushes him into the small plane. The gunmen enter the plane, which then takes off. The helicopter is pushed by the ground crew into a primitive shelter and hidden.

Exterior: Kenya—Small Airport in Early Day

The plane lands in a small private airport. It rapidly taxis to a large hangar. A truck is standing ready. The gunmen rapidly exit the plane and load the tusks on the truck. The plane immediately drives back to the runway and flies away. The gunmen, Jack, and Semi enter the truck and sit by the load of tusks. The truck immediately and swiftly exits the airport area.

Exterior: Kenya—Harbor at Night

The truck enters a small harbor. It stops at the pier. A very large fishing trawler is waiting. The tusks are swiftly loaded into the bottom of the cargo space, packed in large wooden boxes, and hidden in the cargo room. Jack boards the boat. He pushes Semi in front of him. A few crew members immediately release the boat from the pier. The boat leaves the harbor in darkness with no lit lanterns. The truck immediately leaves the harbor area. Jack stands on the deck. Semi is surrounded by fishing nets, boxes, and other equipment. Suddenly, he grasps Semi with both hands and holds him firmly. He lifts him up and holds him at the bulwark. He brutally holds his head so that he faces the water foaming violently under the ship's advance.

JACK, *in Swahili.* You see this water. Shall I push you in?

SEMI, *crying, shaking his head.* Please.

JACK. From now on, you only do as I say. Understood?

SEMI, *shaking and crying.* Yes, always.

JACK. And you never tell anybody what happened!

Semi nods with tears in his eyes. Jack lifts him down on the deck. He holds his hand behind Semi's neck as he guides him over the slippery deck.

JACK. We have a long sail ahead of us. Very, very long.

Jack watches the harbor disappearing behind the ship. He looks down at Semi. Semi looks up at Jack as he loosens his grip and puts his hand on Semi's shoulder. He tightens his lips as to control his thoughts.

JACK. Now ... don't cry. You are safe with me.

Jack and Semi walk over the deck. As they pass a cabin, they hear a noisy conversation between drunken gunmen playing cards. They continue up the deck to the front of the trawler and watch the foaming water as the ship cleaves the waves. They exit the deck to a cabin in the front of the boat.

Exterior: Kenya—Forest in Day

Luno and everyone from the village are walking through the forest to the lake. From the distance they see the piles of dead elephants. They run to the elephants, some of which are still breathing slightly in spite of their terrible wounds. The woman elephant has again move to protect her small but now dead young elephant, which she covers with her last breath. Luno and the crowd shout in grief and fall on their knees around their beloved elephants.

A scream is heard from behind. They turn and see a desperate woman at the hiding place of Semi and Ramo. Luno runs to the place. She finds the headless body of Ramo. She falls to her knees in despair. She rubs the bloody soil on her face while she cries desperately.

LUNO, *crying*. Where is Semi? Where is my son?

Everybody from the village looks around in the forest and at the edge of the savanna. Some women gather around Luno and comfort her in her grief.

Transition to Evening

Exterior: Kenya—Forest in Evening

The sun sets over the savanna. Music fills the space (Nielsen's Second, beginning third movement). The women around Luno help her walk back to the village. The music and the picture fade as they approach the village. The crying of Luno breaks through the music.

Exterior: China—Villa Courtyard in Day

Jack drives his car into the small courtyard in front of his villa. He is casually dressed. Semi is in the back seat dressed in new clothes. Jack steps out of the car. He takes his small luggage from the trunk. He opens the back door of the car, holds Semi's hand, and pulls him gently out of the car. They walk up toward the villa situated above the courtyard. From the entrance to the villa, one oversees the large bay. A major city stretches all along the water and up the mountainsides surrounding the bay. The view is gorgeous. Jack opens the door to the villa and announces his arrival.

JACK, *loud in Mandarin.* I am here. Anybody home?

Semi and Jack enter the villa.

Interior: China—Villa in Day

Jack and Semi enter a small corridor. To the side of the corridor is a door to a large living room. Daylight shines from the living room down the small corridor from panorama windows in the living room. The entire wall of windows provides a total view of the bay and the town. As Jack enters the living room with Semi still behind in the corridor, MIN (who's twenty-five, Chinese, and casually dressed) appears. She immediately embraces Jack.

MIN. So there you are ... finally. I wondered how it could be that long.

She sees Semi.

MIN. But ... what is this?

JACK. He is homeless. We found him on the way.

MIN. Yes, and?

JACK. I thought he could stay here for a while.

MIN. Here ...?

JACK. Yes, and I am sure he can help a bit.

MIN. But how on earth? Does he even speak?

JACK. Not our language but his own. I understand a bit, so he will learn. You can teach him too. And then you have somebody here.

MIN. Have you turned a little crazy on this trip? Maybe because it was so long.

Min loosens her embrace and watches Semi. She takes his hand, pulls him gently to the windows in the living room, and bends down in front of him. She looks him in the eyes as she speaks gently, holding his hand.

MIN. So who are you? What is your name?

Because Semi doesn't understand, Jack addresses him in Swahili.

JACK, *in Swahili.* Say you name!

SEMI, *almost whispering.* Semi.

MIN. So Semi?

SEMI, *nodding and whispering.* Yes.

Min rises, looks puzzled at the panoramic view, and turns back to Jack.

MIN. Are you sure about this? You cannot just pick a child up somewhere and let him be here. And why on earth?

JACK. He is homeless. He is lost. He can be here for a while. I will report him at some point, of course. When he grows up, he may just go back to where he is from—if he knows.

MIN. Okay, but remember that I also have to be out of the house from time to time. I cannot be here all the time.

JACK. Zu will look after him when you need.

Interior: China—Villa in Evening

ZU (who's seventeen and Chinese) serves the evening meal, a traditional noodle soup, for Jack and Min. After serving, she goes to the kitchen in the background. Semi is sitting by a small table in the kitchen. Zu helps him with a spoon for the soup.

MIN. So how was the catch this time?

JACK. It was good, but we have to sail farther and farther away. The fishes are so scarce close to the coast that the trips become longer and longer. (He pauses.) And how is it *over there*?

MIN. Muno is doing better and better. She has become so good in everything I've taught her. (She pauses.) Well, she'd better become clever. They are so rich. So she has to deal with all that comes with that. Wonder how one makes so much money. (She pauses.) Maybe you should ask next time you meet Huang.

Fade to Black

Exterior: China—Villa Huang's Gate during Day

Jack stops his car in front of the heavily guarded gate. Two guards wave him to stop the car. They recognize Jack, open the gate, and wave him through. Jack parks the car right inside the gate and walks up toward the prestigious mansion.

Exterior: China—Villa Huang's Main Door during Day

As Jack reaches the mansion, a servant, GU (who's fifty) already stands in front of the open door. He holds the door open for Jack to enter.

Interior: China—Villa Huang's Lobby during Day

The servant leads Jack through the spacious lobby, which is preciously decorated with classic paintings and sculptures. They reach the office of HUANG (who's fifty). The servant carefully knocks on the door. A voice comes from within. The servant stands aside to let Jack enter.

Interior: China—Villa Huang's Office during Day

As Jack enters the spacious office, Huang rises from his desk and walks toward Jack. The two men meet in the middle of the office. Huang is dressed in business casual dress. He greets Jack in a friendly manner. The two men shake hands.

HUANG, *in Mandarin.* Good to see you. Please take a seat.

Huang points to one of two comfortable, classic chairs in front of his desk. Jack takes his seat while Huang takes the seat opposite by the desk. Two enormous tusks dominate the large classic desk. The room is decorated with classic paintings by French, Austrian, and Dutch artists. In small cabinets throughout the room, small ivory figures are exhibited.

HUANG. Your catch this time was very good. It will generate good money. It is already on the market. Some, of course, is being processed.

JACK. I am glad to hear that.

HUANG. When can you go again? There is a lot of demand right now. We should not miss the opportunity.

JACK. I thought in about six months.

HUANG. I would like you to go before. What about next month? (He pauses.) And by the way, the market for the small ones is particularly attractive these days. You should find more of those!

JACK. Maybe you could make the small ones from the bigger. Then we save the young sources, and we maintain our overall sources better.

HUANG, *in an irritated tone.* No, Jack. I need the real thing. That's where the demand is, and I need it now. So please go next month. This story about maintaining the sources—I don't give a damn! (He pauses.) I will pay you well.

Huang rises and goes to the bookshelves behind his desk. He moves a few books to get access to a safe built into the wall. He dials the code, opens the safe, and takes a thick envelope out. He closes the safe carefully and puts the books in place. He hands Jack the envelope.

HUANG. I added some extras this time. The quality was outstanding. So you can also pay your folks a bit more in the future, if you want. Up to you. And by the way, I have made sure that all your equipment is being upgraded. (He pauses.) Everything is ready for you to go, Jack!

Huang rises and goes over to Jack, who then rises. They shake hands. As they walk together to the exit of the office, Huang pats Jack on the back.

HUANG. By the way, Jack, I am very pleased with Min. Since she started teaching Muno, the progress has been fantastic. She speaks the languages. She understands the mathematics—everything. And Jack, she likes your wife a lot. She asks for her all the time. Good we got that in place.

Jack puts the envelope in his inner pocket. The two men shake hands again. Huang again pats Jack's shoulder. Jack exits.

Interior: China—Villa Huang's Lobby during Day

Gu meets Jack as he exits the office to the lobby. He follows Jack to the front door. Walking through the lobby, Jack briefly watches the small exhibits of precious arts, many made of antique ivory. When they reach the front door, the servant bows politely as Jack exits.

Exterior: China—Villa Huang's Gate during Day

Jack walks swiftly to his car by the gate. A guard opens the car door for Jack. As Jack enters the car, he briefly watches the gorgeous view from the hill of the mansion. A guard opens the gate. Jack drives out and down the steep narrow street.

Exterior: Kenya—Village in Evening

Luno is sitting alone by the fire, waiting. The oldest member of the village, SUNO (who's eighty-five, slim, and tall with gray hair to the shoulders) comes to Luno. They sit face-to-face. The flickering light from the small fire slightly illuminate their faces.

LUNO
Help me. Help me find Semi!

Suno takes Luno's hand and hold them tight. They close their eyes and sit unmoved. On the courtyard by the fires, other families get together.

Transition to Night

Exterior: Kenya—Village at Night

The last family retreats from the courtyard. The fires have burned down to ashes. The sky is black with clear stars. The moon rises and illuminates the courtyard softly with a silver light. Luno and Suno are still motionless. Suno opens his eyes.

SUNO, *whispering*. He is alive. I see him … but far, far away. A place I don't know, but he is alive. (He pauses.) He will come to you again one day.

Luno opens her eyes. They rise and stand for a moment while still holding each other's hands. They separate and walk to their cottages.

Interior: China—Villa during Day

Min and Semi are sitting by a low table in the living room. Min shows him pictures of simple objects and says the word in Mandarin. Semi repeats the words, first silently, but inspired by the smiling and charming Min, he gradually gets encouraged. Their words are heard faintly in the background.

MIN, *pointing at herself.* Me … me.

SEMI, *with difficulty.* Me.

MIN, *pointing at Semi.* You … you.

SEMI, *pointing at Min smiling.* You.

SEMI, *pointing in the direction of Zu.* She—

Transition to Evening

Interior: China—Villa in Evening

Min and Jack are sitting by the low table. There is only little light in the room from a few classic Chinese lamps. Through the panorama windows, the city lights are bright in the clear night. They are having tea. Min fills the cups and hands one to Jack. They speak softly in the quiet evening.

JACK. I have to go again already.

MIN. But why already? You just came back. It was so long.

JACK. Huang likes the boat to be more active. It cannot just be in the harbor for too long. It's too expensive, he says.

MIN, *saddened.* But then have somebody else go. Why always you?

JACK. He does not trust others.

MIN. I don't understand. The harbor is full of boats, and you just leave me so often. And now with Semi. (She pauses.) He is such a cute boy—so clever, so gentle. (She pauses.) But you have to find his parents. They must miss him terribly.

JACK, *looking down while speaking.* They may not want him back. Why should he just be left alone?

MIN. I feel somehow he is so sad. I cheer him up. We make progress. And then suddenly, his thoughts flow away like clouds moving in the wind with no resistance. Too bad he cannot tell me. But he should be able to tell you. You understand his language, at least a bit.

JACK, *hesitates slightly.* Maybe we should not talk about his past if that's what makes him sad. Just let him look forward and forget. That's best for him.

MIN. Okay, if you say so. (She pauses.) At any rate, I will continue to teach him.

Min fills their teacups. They lift the cups to their lips and watch each other lovingly across the gentle vapor.

Exterior: China—Villa's Courtyard during Day

Jack, Min, Semi, and Zu (who's in the background) are in the courtyard. Jack gently kisses Min goodbye and enters the car. He starts driving away. Min waves with one hand while she holds Semi in the other. As the car disappears down the narrow road, Min and Semi walk back to the house hand in hand followed by Zu.

Interior: Kenya—Village Hut at Dawn

Luno is sleeping in the early dawn. A small BOY (who's seven) enters the hut. He shakes Luno by the arm. She wakes up and looks surprised at the boy.

BOY. There are elephants coming again! I hear them—the trumpet.

LUNO. Let's go and see.

The boy wakes up the others in the hut.

LUNO. There are elephants! Come!

They all silently exit the hut.

Exterior: Kenya—Forest at Dawn

The small crowd reaches the lake by the forest. A herd of elephants appears but stops before it reaches the water by the bodies of the dead elephants. They make terrible moaning sounds and flock around the dead. They push the bodies gently with their trunks as if to bring the dead back to life. They stand again, quiet around the dead bodies, shaking their heads and moaning.

While the crew watches the dead elephants in grief, the lead elephant breaks a large branch from a tree and places it over the dead bodies. All the other elephants follow suit and break branches from the trees. Before long, all the dead bodies are neatly buried below large piles of branches and leaves. The elephants again flock around the dead with moaning sounds. Finally, the lead elephant goes to the water. All the other elephants follow. They drink and bath but without the delighted sounds of the extinguished herd.

Finally, the lead elephant walks away from the lake to the edge of the savanna. The herd slowly follows and disappears. The small crew from the village follows the elephants to get one last glimpse of the animals. They turn and walk back to the village hand in hand, forming a chain to comfort one another.

Interior: China—Villa during Day

Min and Semi are sitting side by side at the low table on a rainy day. Min holds a children's book with pictures of animals, one on each page, and she is teaching Semi the names of the animals one by one.

MIN. Hen.

SEMI. Hen. Hen. Hen!

MIN, *correcting the pronunciation.* Hen.

SEMI, *upbeat.* Hen.

MIN. Great. Now let's turn the page.

Min turns the page.

Min. Bird.

SEMI. Bird.

MIN. Great. And the next.

Min turns the page.

Min. Fish.

SEMI. Fish!

They both smile. Semi is making good progress. Min moves a little closer to Semi and again turns the page.

MIN. Elephant.

Semi sits motionless and looks at the picture of a small elephant.
MIN. Elephant. You can say it. Come.

Semi remains motionless. Min turns to look him directly in the eyes. She sees Semi's eyes filled with tears. Semi is desperately trying to avoid crying. Min puts her arm around Semi to comfort him.

MIN. What is it? Tell me.

Semi remains motionless. Suddenly, he rises and runs to the windows and goes out through the terrace door. Min rises and watches Semi running to a small bush at the edge. He sits behind the bush and hides.

Exterior: China—Villa Terrace during Day

Min walks out on the terrace and over to the small bush where Semi is hiding. She kneels down next to him.

MIN. Come!

Semi remains sitting, motionless. Min touches him gently and puts her arm around him with great tenderness.

MIN. Come!

Min takes Semi's hand. They both rise and walk hand in hand back to the terrace door. They exit the terrace.

Interior: China—Villa Huang's Office during Day

Huang and Jack are in the office. Huang, clearly dismayed, is sitting by the desk. Jack is sitting in one of the chairs facing the desk.

HUANG, *extremely angry.* How on earth could that happen? You are supposed to have the whole route cleared!

JACK. I did, and we paid handsomely. Very handsomely actually. Everything agreed.

HUANG. Well, obviously, you don't know well enough what you are doing ... and even so close to ourselves. (He pauses.) A stupid inspection!

JACK. I believe there is a new supervisor down there.

Huang, extremely upset, hammers his hands in the desk and stands up, leaning forward with both hands on the desk. His expression is evil.

HUANG. You say you think there is a new supervisor. You are not supposed to think. You are supposed to know. Your ignorance threatened our entire secure route.

Huang walks over to Jack. He takes a seat next to Jack in the second chair facing the desk. He controls himself as he leans close to Jack, talking softly.

HUANG. Here is what you have to do.

Interior: China—Villa in Evening

Min, who is dressed in modern yet traditional dress, and Jack are sitting by the low table. Min is making the tea. She hands Jack his cup. They both lift their cups to enjoy the flavor. Their eyes meet through the gentle steam from the cups.

MIN. It was so long again, dear.

JACK. We have to get so far. And we had some difficulty with the machine.

MIN. Please don't be away so long anymore. When I see the clouds flying with the wind, I see you so distant. (She pauses.) I see the clouds flow in the irresistible wind to the horizon, and there they dissolve.

She pours fresh tea in their cups. She lifts her cup to the lips and speaks through the gentle vapor and fragrance.

MIN. And what can the clouds do but go with the wind? There is no way for a cloud to resist the wind until it finally dissolves and disappears forever.

Min puts her cup on the table. She watches the cup and the table with sad eyes as she puts her hands on her lap. Jack holds his cup up to his face while he watches Min. She looks up, and their eyes meet.

MIN. Semi has been very sad sometimes.

JACK. And?

MIN. I learned him the names of the animals. He was doing so well. As always. (She pauses and speaks quietly.) He is so clever and cute.

Min looks down while she hesitates to continue. She composes herself and again looks Jack in the eyes.

MIN. When we came to the elephant in the book, he just did not want to learn. He cried and went to the terrace ... out there. He was hiding. (She pauses.) I don't know why. He still knows so few words, so we cannot really talk. (She pauses.) Maybe you can try to understand.

JACK. I think it is better just to look forward. We don't know his past. Maybe it's best that he not think and talk about it.

Min and Jack remain sitting for a while. They rise. Before they exit, they briefly pull the curtain aside to the room where Semi is sleeping. Semi is lying on his side. In his arms he holds the book open to the picture of the small elephant. He embraces the book and holds it close to his heart. Min and Jack stand still for a moment and watch. Min's eyes become wet. Jack looks down as Min tries to capture his sight.

MIN, *whispering*. What is going on, dear?

Jack shakes his head. They let the curtain fall gently. They exit the room.

Exterior: China—Villa Huang's Main Door during Day

Min walks up the stairs to the front door of the impressive mansion. The servant GU (who's fifty, Chinese, and slim with gray hair) stands in the door and holds it open for Min to enter. The two know each other well.

MIN. Thanks, Gu. Is she ready?

GU, *smiling.* She has been talking about you all morning!

MIN. Wonderful. She is doing so well.

Interior: China—Villa Huang's Lobby during Day

Min enters the foyer. MUNO (a nine-year-old Chinese girl who's cutely dressed) run through the foyer to Min. She bends down to face Muno.

MIN. Morning, Muno. Are you ready?

MUNO, *jumping happily.* Yes!

Muno takes Min's hand and almost pulls her through the foyer

to the door of the library.

Interior: China—Villa Huang's Library during Day

Min and Muno enter the library, which is richly decorated with books and arts on all of the walls. They take seats by a large table in the middle of the room. Muno's books are at the table. Min takes her notebook from her handbag.

MIN. Now first show me all the signs you have made for today.

Muno proudly takes a sheet from her notes. She pushes it over to Min, who admires the neatly made signs.

MIN. This is very nice. Just look here.

Min places the paper between them on the table and makes a few corrections while Muno watches attentively.

MIN. Now it's fine. And now you show me you can read this.

Min takes a sheet of paper and puts it on the middle of the table. Muno reads it with some difficulty.

MUNO. The clouds ... are in the sky. The rain is in the clouds ... The rain—

Muno is interrupted as someone abruptly opens the door to the library. Her mother, DAIYU (who's thirty), quickly enters the room. She's dressed in high-fashion clothes and wearing obviously expensive jewelry. As she enters, Min and Muno both rise and stand straight up by their chairs. Muno is clearly anxious.

DAIYU. Is she making any progress?

She grabs the sheet with the corrected signs on the table.

DAIYU. So you had to make all these corrections?

MUNO. Yes, but they were all very minor. She has—

DAIYU, *interrupting Min.* This is not good. So many corrections. You are a lazy girl.

Daiyu tears the paper up and throws it on the floor in front of Muno, who stands straight and looks down on the floor.

DAIYU. You have to be tougher to her. We pay you to move her forward, not backward.

MIN. Yes, of course, but—

DAIYU, *interrupting in an irritated tone.* Next time there shall be no mistakes!

Daiyu quickly turns around and exits the room, slamming the door. Muno stands with tears in her eyes. Min runs to her and bends down to comfort her.

Interior: China—Villa Huang's Lobby during Day

Irritated, Daiyo walks swiftly from the library, crosses the lobby, and goes to the office. She opens the door and enters without knocking.

Interior: China—Villa Huang's Office during Day

Huang is sitting at his desk. Daiyu walks up to the desk and stands opposite Huang.

DAIYU. Why do we continue to have this woman in the house?

HUANG, *rising in an irritated way.* I told you. She is a good teacher, and Muno is making wonderful progress—in all respects.

DAIYU. Is that what you call progress? Plenty of mistakes on even the simplest characters. I just looked. It was miserable!

HUANG. Well, what exactly—

DAIYU, *interrupting.* You must be blind. I don't want this woman in my house anymore. Get her out! We should not have foreign people here at any rate. She can do the teaching in her house. It's nearby. Of course I know she is important for you. Well, they both are.

HUANG. It should work at her place too—as long as it is safe.

Huang sits down by the desk.

HUANG. Well, okay then. I just need a couple of bodyguards joining to protect her as long as she is so young, just in case. We don't want to come under pressure. You know what I mean.

DAIYU. I will tell her.

Daiyu starts walking to the exit.

DAIYU. I am going to visit Fang. I will be there all afternoon.

HUANG. Please mention that we had a few issues in the harbor recently. He must do something. There must be no delays. Our loads have to be completely fresh.

DAIYU, *irritated*. How did that happen?

HUANG. There is a new manager. We are dealing with it, but you'd better mention it anyway. And please remind him … you know.

Daiyu turns around and swiftly exits the office.

Exterior: China—Villa Huang's Main Door during Day

Daiyu exits the front door. A Bentley is waiting. The driver stands by the open door to the car. Daiyu enters. The driver closes the door and enters the front door. The car immediately drives out of the courtyard.

Exterior: China—Harbor during Day

Jack walks along the many small fishing boats and trawlers in the busy harbor. He continues up to a small administration buildings. He enters.

Interior: China—Guon's Office at Harbor during Day

GUON (who's fifty, Chinese, and a small tight man) is sitting by his desk in the messy office. His telephone rings.

GUON. Yes?

WOMAN'S VOICE, *nervous.* It's me.

GUON. So what's up?

WOMAN'S VOICE. Did you pick Biyu up?

GUON. No. Why?

WOMAN'S VOICE. She was not there when I came to pick her.

GUON. So where is she then?

WOMAN'S VOICE, *crying.* I just don't know. I asked everybody there.

GUON. Please go again. Call if you don't find her.

Guon hangs up. Jack enters the office.

JACK. Do you have a moment?

GUON. Well, could it wait please. There is something I urgently need to deal with.

JACK. Is anything wrong?

GUON. Well, somehow my daughter was not where she used to be. My wife was supposed to pick her up.

JACK. Well, my friend, I'm sure she'll turn up. But you'd better take care. This won't happen again, right?

The telephone rings.

GUON. Excuse me. Let me just answer.

Guon picks up the phone.

GUON. Hello?

WOMAN'S VOICE. I found her!

GUON. So where was she?

WOMAN'S VOICE. Apparently, over behind the school on some kind of a new playground.

GUON, *relieved.* Good. I will be back as usual.

Guon hangs up the phone. Jack moves closer to the desk and looks very directly at Guon.

JACK. This won't happen again, right? (He pauses.) My friend, lately we've had some delays when our boat landed. You know how important that is for us. Our catch has to be absolutely fresh for the market.

GUON. I understand.

JACK. I'd like to pay an extra fee to make sure we have a smooth pass. Maybe you could clear us yourself in the future.

Jack hands Guon an envelope.

JACK. We will pay regular fees. I will be in touch from time to time. (He pauses.) So take care. Also take good care of your daughter.

Jack rises and exits. Guon puts the envelope away. His telephone rings.

GUON. Yes?

MALE'S VOICE, *angry.* I had a complaint about you! You have been delaying cargoes.

GUON. I'm sorry. We have—

MALE'S VOICE, *interrupting in an irritated tone.* You know what to do, and you know what I am talking about, right? Don't let me ever hear about this again!

The man hangs up.

Interior: Kenya—Helicopter at Dawn

Jack and his men in the helicopter are preparing their weapons as they fly low over the savanna. In the distance they see a herd of elephants. As they get closer, they see the large lead elephant and numerous baby elephants walking behind their mothers. Jack watches with concern as they open the doors in preparation of shooting them.

JACK. This time don't hit the small ones and the mothers ... and not the lead.

GUNMAN 1. Then we will get almost nothing!

JACK. Just do as I say!

The shooting starts. Shortly afterward, the helicopter lands. The gunmen rush out on the savanna. Jack sits back, hiding his head in the hands as the shooting continues and the sound of trumpeting, saws, and axes fills the air.

Interior: China—Villa Huang's Office in Evening

Huang, Jack, Daiyu, and WEI (who's fifty-five) are in the office. Wei, a rough, tight, well-fed financial manager, is sitting opposite Huang by the desk with a pile of papers. Daiyu is standing a bit farther from the desk. Jack is sitting next to Wei opposite Huang. Huang is smoking a cigarette. Daiyu is also smoking but with a cigarette smoking tube, which she holds with two fingers, and puffs small shapes of smoke into the office space. Wei and Jack are having whiskey. Irritated, Huang moves around in his chair as he reads through the documents on the desk.

HUANG. It is not good enough! I asked for increased revenues, and you tell me we are barely keeping what we have. What's going on?

WEI. Well, from my perspective it is pretty simple. On the retail end, you are losing ground to your main competitor.

HUANG, *interrupting in an irritated tone*. You mean Qi, right?
WEI. Yes, I mean—

HUANG. Then say Qi for Christ's sake. We need action and clarity, not some vague talk, right? And what else?

WEI. Well, on the supply side, we get less and less.

Wei looks at Jack, who rises and goes to the small buffet with bottles of whiskey and other beverages. He fills his glass half up and takes a big gulp.

JACK. It's getting more and more difficult. The police are on the ground, and Qi is there as well.

HUANG. What do you mean that Qi is there as well? Tell me what's going on!

JACK. Well, Qi has established his people across large areas. We cannot get in there. He has an army on the ground. (He pauses.) And we have the police in other places too. They're pretty well armed, and they're focusing a lot on our best areas.

HUANG. But Qi must have the same problems.

JACK. I think he has some kind of agreement.

Huang rises in explosive anger and hammers his hands in the desk.

HUANG. Why am I only hearing about this now? And why aren't I hearing about what we can do about it? (He turns to Daiyu.) What about you? Any progress?

DAIYU. I am only missing one more certain vote.

HUANG. Okay, you tell Wei where we can get that vote, and then Wei, you make that happen whatever the cost. What else, folks?

WEI. Let me look into the finances of Qi again. I have someone in his camp. (He pauses, looks over at Jack.) I will need some help from you here on the ground as well. There's gonna be some pressure!

They all rise and go to the exit. Daiyu talks softly to Wei. He nods. They exit the office.

Exterior: China—Villa Courtyard in Evening

Wei and Jack exit the front door. A car with a driver is waiting for Wei. They stand briefly by the car. Wei puts his arm around the shoulders of Jack and whispers a few words. He enters the car. The driver closes the door and drives to the gate. The guards open the gate. Jack walks to his car, which is parked by the gate. He enters the car and drives down the narrow street.

Interior: China—Villa during Day

Min is sitting by the low table. Semi is drawing on a sheet of paper. Muno knocks softly on the door from the outside. Min walks rapidly over and opens. Muno is standing outside, carrying her notebooks. The driver and two bodyguards are standing behind her.

MIN. Come, Muno!

She takes Muno's hand. The driver goes back to the car. The two bodyguards walk around the house. One stands outside of the window at the terrace. The other walks to the front of the house. Muno sees Semi. Their eyes meet. Semi looks down. Min waves for him to come closer.

MIN. Say hello to Muno. She will come here to learn every day.
MUNO. Hello!

SEMI, *very low.* Hello.

Muno stretches her hand out to Semi and presents herself politely. He takes her hand. He retreats to the back of the room and continues drawing. Min starts the lesson with Muno. The bodyguard on the terrace finds a comfortable chair and sits down to enjoy the view.

Interior: Europe—Conference Center during Day

The large conference hall is packed with delegates from all over the world. Twenty panel members are situated near the podium. On the wall behind the panel members, a sign with large letters says, "The Annual World Wildlife Conference." Daiyu is sitting among the panel members, conversing with an African delegate sitting to her side. The CHAIRMAN (who's sixty, Swedish, fit, tall, and well built) of the conference rises and goes to the lectern. He addresses the delegates.

CHAIRMAN, *in English.* I am very pleased to welcome you all to our yearly assembly. And I am delighted to see the massive representation today from all over the world. I am pleased as it shows me how the urgency of our mission is appreciated worldwide. The urgency of preserving the life of our planet has never been greater. You will learn the depressing statistics during this conference. The urgency of our task is enormous. (He pauses.) But let me first share with you some exiting news. Our executive committee met yesterday to nominate our new chairman for the next period. As you know, I will retire. And let me share with you the wonderful news. Our new chairman will be Daiyu Zun.

The chairman applauds, and all of the delegates follow his lead. Daiyu stands and goes to the chairman. He embraces her under the continuing applaud. Daiyu addresses the delegates from the lectern.

DAIYU. Thank you, Mr. Chairman, and thanks to all of you for the great confidence you have shown me.

Delegates applaud.

DAIYU. I can assure you—and this is my promise to you all—that I will dedicate all my time and efforts to the fight for our endangered species. Never before has this fight been more urgent. The rule of law is being displaced by terrible forces throughout the world, and the challenges to fight back because of our limited resources are enormous. Our limited forces cannot even get to some areas where crimes are being committed as we speak. (She pauses.) What I will promise you is that no place will be controlled by unscrupulous gangs. Everywhere our folks on the ground will have access, and with them will come rule and order.

Delegates applaud.

DAIYU. With that, let me introduce the first speaker.

Cross Fade

Interior: China—Restaurant's Private Room—Evening

Huang, Wei, and QI (who's fifty-five) are in a restaurant's private room. Female servants are clearing the low table and serving tea. The three men wait for the servants to leave the room. Qi is a tough-looking, tight, muscular but small character with the eyes of a snake. He looks at Huang, waiting for his comments.

HUANG. My good friend, let me be direct and open with you. You are in deep trouble.

QI. Really?

HUANG. You know, my friend, how people look at tax evasions these days, right? Even the slightest discrepancy and you go to jail.

QI. Sure, but what has that got to do with me? Look, Huang, I agreed to come here because I thought you had some interesting proposals to make. And now you just talk about my taxes.

HUANG. We know about your latest transactions, and my good friend, we actually have a proposal for you.

QI. Let me hear.

HUANG. We buy your business, and in return, the information we have goes no further.

Qi furiously hammers his hands in the table.

QI. Stop your insults, Huang. You know very well that you are losing ground in this business. My people have control on the ground, and on the retail side, we have totally hammered you out. You have less and less. You know that. And yet you come here and make ridiculous proposals because you claim to have information about my taxes.

Qi rises. Huang and Wei rise.

HUANG. Let me know if you change your mind.

QI, *with contempt.* Goodbye, old friend!

Qi exits. Huang and Wei remain standing.

Exterior: Kenya—Forest at Night

A row of lorries drive through the forest and stops at the border of the forest and the savanna. About fifty government troopers jump of the lorries. The LEAD TROOPER (who's thirty) shows the direction to the men. They spread out and hide in the forest. The lead trooper and the men are heavily armed and possess mobile devices. The lorries drive away, leaving the men in total silence.

Exterior: Kenya—Forest at Dawn

Two old lorries, which are loaded with gunmen, and an empty truck enter the area. They stop close to the border of the savanna. The men gather and walk silently down to a small lake and hide. Silence fills the area.

The trumpeting of an elephant is heard. The gunmen ready their heavy weapons. The lead elephant approaches the small lake. Behind the huge male elephant, there's a herd of twenty elephants with the small elephants holding the tails of their mothers as they follow. When the elephants come close enough, the gunmen rise and take sight of the elephants. The lead elephant sees the gunmen and trumpets loud. In that moment, the shooting starts. The gunmen fall one after the other as the troopers shoot. Some gunmen flee back to their trucks.

LEAD TROOPER, *shouting*. Stop. Throw down your weapons.

The gunmen continue their flight and start shooting at the troopers. The troopers return fire. All of the gunmen are killed. The lead trooper walks from gunman to gunman lying on the ground. His men gather the bodies.

The lead trooper calls for assistance over his phone. The trucks arrive. The bodies of the gunmen are loaded on the trucks. The men gather and walk toward the elephants. The lead elephant looks at the lead trooper. He walks slowly toward the elephant without his weapons. The elephant trumpets and waves its head gently from side to side. The lead trooper goes all the way to the elephant. The animal stretches its trunk toward the trooper. He gently touches it. He looks the elephant in its eyes. The elephant turns around and walks back to the herd, which is now drinking by the lake. The men go to the lorries and drive away as the sun breaks through the forest.

Exterior: Kenya—Forest in Evening

About fifty government troopers are silently surrounding a few primitive buildings deep in the forest. They take positions all around the buildings and make their weapons ready. The lead trooper shouts toward the building.

LEAD TROOPER. You are surrounded. Throw down your weapons and come out.

The troopers hear the gunmen readying their weapons. The gunmen inside the building start firing at the troopers. The troopers return fire with heavy weapons. The building is blown to pieces, and all of gunmen are shot to death. The lead trooper approaches the building. He walks from body to body with his weapon ready. He calls for assistance over the phone. Three trolleys arrive. The gunmen and their weapons are loaded up. The lorries drive away. The troopers gather next to the building.

LEAD TROOPER. Good job, folks. The area is cleared!

The lead trooper walks from man to man and shakes their hands. The tough men smile, relieved. They all step up on the last trolley and drive away.

Exterior: China—Villa Qi's Gate at Night

Five police cars reach the heavily guarded gate by Qi's mansion. The police officers and heavily armed men walk to the gate and shoot the locks open. The guards are immediately held up by the police. The cars drive fast up to the mansion.

Exterior: China—Villa Qi's Courtyard at Night

The police cars stop by the front door. The men quickly surround the house. A frightened Chinese servant opens the door. The police run into the house.

Shortly afterward, a police officer appears with Qi in chains. He is pushed into a police car, and they immediately drive away. Numerous police officers enter the building. Light shines in all windows. Police officers carry stacks of paper and electronic equipment out of the house and load the material into the police cars.

Exterior: Kenya—Forest at Night

Three trucks arrive at the remains of the buildings. Jack and six men jump down from the truck and walk up to the ruins. They carefully search the whole building. Jack finds a metal cover at the floor of the ruins. He calls his helpers.

JACK. Break this one up.

The men collect tools from the trucks and break the metal cover open. An entry to an underground room becomes visible. Jack takes a flashlight out and crawls down in the underground room.

Interior: Kenya—Underground Room in Forest at Night

Jack enters the underground room. The spacious room is filled with wooden boxes. He calls out to his men. Three men come to Jack with tools. They break a wooden box open and find large elephant tusks. They close the box again and hammer it tightly closed with the nails.

JACK. Get it all on the trucks.

The men empty the underground room and load the numerous boxes on the trucks. They carefully reposition the metal door and hide it under rubble. They go to the trucks and drive away.

Exterior: Kenya—Harbor at Night

Jack stands at the pier next to the fishing trawler. His men load the wooden boxes onto the ship and take them down in the cargo room. Jack goes on board. The ship silently leaves the harbor.

Interior: China—Law Office in Evening

Huang, Wei, and Qi's attorney sits by a small conference table in the messy office. QI'S ATTORNEY (who's fifty and slim with gray hair and wearing business attire) is holding a single piece of paper. He hands it to Huang, who hands it to Wei. He briefly reads through the short document.

WEI, *addressing Huang.* It is as agreed.

HUANG. Very well then.

Huang pushes the paper over to the attorney. He signs and hands the paper back to Huang, who takes the paper and hands it to Wei. The men rise.

HUANG. Please remind my old friend that this trouble could have been avoided.

Huang and Wei exit the office.

Interior: China—Villa during Day

Min is teaching Muno in the living room. They go carefully through sheets with signs. Min makes a few corrections. The bodyguards stand outside of the house at their usual places. Semi, who's less shy now, is close enough to follow the lesson. While listening, he makes small drawings. From time to time, Min shows him the signs. When she has corrected one sheet, she gives it to Semi to look at.

MIN. It is very good now. So few things for me to correct. So now let's try some reading.

She hands Muno a sheet from a small pile of paper. Muno looks through the signs on the sheet. She looks at Semi. She's smiling and proud as she starts reading.

MUNO. The rain in the forests makes everybody seek shelter. The birds hide under the large leaves.

The sound fades.

Cross Fade to Nine Years Later

Exterior: China—Street Restaurant during Day

Semi (who's now eighteen) is sitting by a small table in a busy street, waiting. He enjoys a cup of tea while drawing on his sketchbook. From time to time, he looks up, slightly impatient.

Muno is running up the street, carrying her study material. When Semi sees her, he rises and waves. Muno sees him and quickly comes to the table. She puts her study material on an empty chair next to her. She smiles lovingly to Semi and briefly puts her hand on his. She is upbeat and full of energy.

MUNO, *in Mandarin.* This lecture went on and on. It seemed he would never stop. (She pauses.) But now I am here.

Muno touches Semi's hand again. He puts his sketchbook at the table. A servant shows up. Muno moves back in the chair.

MUNO. Just some tea please!

The servant walks away. Muno moves close to the table. MUNO. So how was it today?

SEMI, *in Mandarin.* This professor is so good. I could listen to him all the time. We make drawings, and he corrects us I tell you … he really knows his stuff.

MUNO. Can I see?

Muno takes the sketchbook and looks through the pictures. The servant serves her tea. Semi watches her anxiously as she browses through the pages. Muno looks over at Semi while she takes a sip from her tea.

MUNO. Who is that girl?

SEMI. I don't know. She is just the model we all draw.

MUNO. Well, is that really how she looks? Or is it how you see her?

SEMI. It should be both. That's the whole idea.

MUNO. You should draw me. Then I can see where your heart is.

Muno smiles with a bit of sadness as she looks lovingly at Semi.

SEMI. Let me try. Give me the book. Just sit like that. Just like that.

Semi quickly makes a drawing of Muno, emphasizing her loving and caring eyes.

MUNO. May I see?

Semi hands her the sketchbook.

MUNO. Maybe I mean a bit to you after all.

Muno sits quietly for a little while, drinking her tea. Charmed, she looks at Semi.

MUNO. I have a proposal for you. (She pauses.) Will you just listen?

SEMI, *smiling*. Of course. What is it?

MUNO. Well, since you've never proposition me, I'll make one for you.

Muno lowers her voice.

MUNO. You see, there is nobody in the house tomorrow—nobody. So we could have dinner here in town, and we could be together in the house afterward. What do you say?

SEMI. But we cannot do that? Imagine what could happen. The guards at the gate are always there. They will know what's going on.

MUNO. I know how to deal with that.

They sit in silence.

MUNO. Please.

SEMI. Okay then.

Muno rises, delighted. She gathers her things and stands for a short moment by the table, making a sensual and loving impression. She walks down the street, waving without turning around.

Interior: China—Restaurant in Evening

Muno and Semi sit at a small table outside of a restaurant. A happy RESTAURANT OWNER places many small bowels with a wide variety of dishes on the table. Muno wears delicate makeup, and she is dressed in modern clothes this warm evening. She samples all of the small dishes. Semi is worried about the situation, but gradually, he goes with the flow and follows Muno's excitement and energy.

SEMI. I finished the drawing. Would you like to see it?

MUNO, *excited.* Show me. Show me.

Semi takes the rolled-up drawing from under his shirt. He hands the roll to Muno. She unrolls it, gazed at it for a short moment, and looks at Semi with an excited expression.

MUNO. Maybe you like me at least as much as you like your model.

SEMI. If that's what you see, you read my mind.

MUNO. I will keep it forever. Forever and forever. You know that, right? (She pauses.) I think we are done!

As if puzzled, Muno looks at Semi.

MUNO. Come!

They rise and exit.

Exterior: China—Villa Huang's Back Gate in Evening

Muno and Semi walk by the back of the mansion. They stop by a small metal door in the wall surrounding the mansion. Muno smiles to Semi. She takes a key from her bag. The door opens with a creaking sound. Muno puts her finger across her lips to encourage silence. She takes Semi by the hand and walks through the door. She shuts the door silently. They walk through the back garden by means of a small path between high bushes, and they come to a door on the backside of the mansion. Muno unlocks the door. Again, she takes Semi by the hand and enters the house.

Interior: China—Villa Huang's Kitchen in Evening

Muno and Semi enter the kitchen through the back door. Muno quickly closes the door and takes Semi by the hand.

MUNO. You see, it's not so difficult to get in here!

Semi looks around the spacious kitchen.

SEMI. Wow, this isn't my small kitchen in the college.

MUNO, *pulling Semi to a side door.* Come!

Interior: China—Muno's Room in Villa Huang in Evening

Muno and Semi enter Muno's room. The room is classically furnished and decorated with Chinese pieces, but it's a bit messy with Muno's clothes, cosmetics, papers, and books all over the place. Muno lovingly grasps a large silk cover, and while holding the cover in one hand, she embraces Semi fully. They turn around and around while they engage in a deep and lasting kiss. The silk cover flies around them above their heads, and as they slow down, the cover wraps them together. Wrapped together in the silk cover, they fall on the bed and make love.

Exterior: China—Pier at Harbor

The large fishing trawler reaches the pier. Jack gets off and meets Guon at the pier. They shake hands. Guon goes on board with Jack. They walk up and down the deck. Jack hands Guon some papers for his signature. Guon signs, and the two men shake hands again. Guon walks back to the pier.

Three large trucks drive up to the pier. Jack's men immediately start loading the trucks with the large wooden boxes. When loaded, the trucks drive away. Jack leaves the ship and walks up the pier, tired and worried. As he reaches his car, which is parked close to the pier by a small administration building, he stands there for a while. He hides his head in his hands. Finally, he enters the car and drives away.

Exterior: China—Shopping Street during Day

Muno and Semi are walking down the busy, narrow shopping street. Muno holds Semi's arm and leans as close to Semi as appropriate without showing her total love and dedication. They pass a jewelry shop. Sumo pulls Semi to the window, which displays beautiful jewelry. Muno pulls Semi a little closer, smiling.

MUNO. Let's go in and find something. Something for me perhaps?

SEMI. But the money. You know that's not my strong side.

MUNO. Here is what we do. I buy something to give to you as a gift to give to me as a gift.

Muno pulls herself close to Semi. They enter the shop.

Interior: China—Jewelry Shop during Day

Muno and Semi enter the small jewelry shop. Muno tightly holds Semi's arm. The SHOP OWNER (who's sixty, slim, and Chinese with gray hair and traditionally dress) is sitting in the corner of the shop by a small desk. As Muno and Semi enter the shop, he rises and goes to the small counter.

SHOP OWNER. What can I do for you?

MUNO. Can we just look around please?

SHOP OWNER. Of course. Just let me know if I can do something for you.

Muno and Semi walk around the shop and look at all of the well-organized cabinets and exhibits. Muno stops by the cabinet with rings. She points at a ring with a moonstone.

MUNO. I like that one. It's like the light during the evening.

SEMI. It is beautiful, but—

MUNO, *interrupting.* Let's ask him to take it out.

Muno turns to the shop owner.

MUNO. Can we see this one please?

SHOP OWNER. Of course.

The shop owner takes a bundle of small keys from a drawer below one of the counters. He walks over to Muno and Semi, unlocks the cabinet, and takes out the ring. As he moves it, the ring reflects small rays of silver light. He cleans the ring carefully with a soft cloth and hands it to Muno. She takes the ring and hands it to Semi.

MUNO. Please try it on me. See if it fits!

Muno holds her left hand with the fingers spread forward. Semi pushes the ring on her finger. The fit is perfect. Muno jumps a little in happiness, leans toward Semi, and looks lovingly at him.

MUNO. I like it. Do you like it?

SEMI. Totally.

SHOP OWNER. It certainly looks very good on you.

MUNO. Can we buy it please?

SHOP OWNER. Of course. Do you want me to pack it for you?

MUNO. Please.

The shop owner puts the ring in a small duvet box. Muno pays with her golden credit card. She puts the small package in Semi's pocket. They exit the shop.

Exterior: China—Shopping Street during Day

Muno and Semi walk down the shopping street. They stop by a small cafe and take two seats by a table in the open. A servant comes to the table.

MUNO. Tea for two please.

The servant walks away. Muno looks at Semi with great expectation.

MUNO. Maybe you have a gift for me after last night?

Semi smiles and takes the small box with the ring from his pocket. He gives it to Muno. She opens the box and admires the ring. She hands the open box back to Semi. He takes the ring out of the box. Muno puts her hand on the table. Semi puts the ring on her finger. Muno kisses the ring on her finger, the stone flickering in the light. She takes both hands close to her heart and looks lovingly at Semi. The waiter brings tea for two.

Interior: China—Villa Huang's Office in Evening

Huang, Wei, Jack, and Daiyu are in the office. Huang sits at his desk and reads through a short report with obvious dismay. Daiyu smokes a cigarette using her cigarette holder while barely touching either the cigarette or the fume. She leans against the wall. Wei sits opposite Huang by the desk. He checks a single attachment in a large pile of papers. Jack stands by the buffet with a whiskey.

HUANG. Revenues are good, but why are supplies again dropping?

WEI. Revenues are good because of demand and our control now of the majority of the retail. Almost every family today wants a piece, so we can ask really good prices. In fact, the prices are through the roof at some places. And we can control them to a large extent. (He pauses.) Supplies—I don't know. It seems particularly the small ones are lacking.

They all look at Jack.

HUANG, *irritated.* So Jack, what's going on?

JACK. It's just getting more and more difficult. There's simply not much anymore. And what is there is more spread out.

DAIYU. Jack, there is some truth to what you say, but the statistics I have from the organization do not suggest such a drop. Some drop, yes, but not so much. No way.

JACK. Maybe. But the spread of the source over large areas is a fact, so we simply need more and more time.

Huang gets extremely upset. He stands and keeps his hands on the desk while he talks.

HUANG. But then take more time. We have a business to take care of here. A business needs supplies, right! So get the supplies for us. You just heard what Daiyu said. And if you need more trips, then take more trips. If you need more people, well then ask for more people. It is very simple.

Huang looks over at Daiyu as he continues.

HUANG. What about clearing other areas?

DAIYU. Yes, there are area where the government forces are stretched and where a few groups gain some foothold. I could manage that, but then Jack will need additional force to fill the space when I get it cleared and follow up so that we don't lose it again.

HUANG. Let's do that. Jack, build up for that. It means a full additional chain, I suppose. And Wei, free up the resources. We will take some hits on next year's profits.

WEI. There's one more thing we can do perhaps. I see more and more goods enter from small opportunistic individuals. There is an increasing black market!

HUANG. It is very simple! Jack, get rid of them, and then get their goods. They probably have plenty. What are you waiting for? Keep some of your folks on the ground and get more men we can trust. And Daiyu—

DAIYU, *interrupting.* Yes, I'll push for more forces to help clear the ground. Then Jack can get in.

Cross Fade

Exterior: Kenya—Forest at Night

A small group of poachers are sitting around a fire in the forest next close to the savanna. Their weapons and equipment are piled up around them. Suddenly, a large number of Jack's men appear all around the poachers. They immediately start shooting. The poachers rise to get to their weapons. A few starts returning fire. All of the men are gunned down within a few minutes. Jack's men walk around the bodies and shoot anyone showing sign of life through the head. They gather the poachers' weapons and disappear in the forest.

Cross Fade

Interior: Europe—Conference Center during Day

The delegates of the Annual Wildlife Conference are mingling at an informal get-together. Daiyu is assisted by a few high-ranking coworkers from the organization, and she walks from delegate to delegate for informal conversations. One by one the delegates, flattered by Daiyu's interest, nod as she touches them and expressed her confidence.

Exterior: China—Street Restaurant during Day

Muno and Semi are seated by a small outdoor table near the sidewalk. Muno is holding her tea up to her lips with both hands. The light flashes in her ring and eyes.

MUNO. I have the house all to myself for a couple of days. Are you very busy?

Semi shakes his head.

MUNO. Bring your drawing paper please. Make me a new drawing.

Cross Fade

Interior: China—Muno's Roon in Villa Huang in Evening

Muno and Semi are in Muno's room. Muno is sitting on the bed with the silk cover around her naked body. Semi sits under a cover by the end of the bed, finishing a drawing. Muno stretches her hand toward him. He hands her the drawing. She looks at it with love.

MUNO. Do I see that you love me deeply?

SEMI. The picture is from the bottom of my soul.

Muno moves down to the bed end with the silk cover still around her naked body. As she lifts her arms and holds them around Semi's neck to give him a deep kiss, the silk cover slides down. Semi holds her naked back. Muno rises and puts the silk cover around her body.

MUNO. Let's make some food. There's nobody in the house.

They rise. Muno holds the silk cover around her body. They exit.

Interior: China—Villa Huang's Kitchen in Evening

Muno and Semi are sitting by a table in the kitchen, sharing a few fruits. Semi cuts the fruits with a large kitchen knife.

MUNO. Do you think we can be together for good?

SEMI. But what about your family? They probably have big plans for you, and I am just nothing. I'm from a different world. I don't even know who I am.

MUNO. How can you say you are nothing? You are everything. So deep. (She pauses.) If anyone is nothing, it's me. Look at my life. Looks like I have everything, right? But love? Mother. Father maybe. The only person who really cares is Min ... and you perhaps. (She pauses.) So I don't care what they think. Maybe I should tell Father about you.

SEMI. But what if he gets angry and something happens to Min and Jack? Maybe wait a little, at least until I have finished the studies. It'll be soon, you know.

MUNO. Okay, but you know what I want. Do you know what you want? Do you want me?

SEMI. Of course.

MUNO. And nothing else?

SEMI. Never.

Muno rises, moves to Semi, sits on his lap, and embraces him.

MUNO. Let's celebrate. Just a small glass. I know there are bottles in the office. Come!

Muno rises, holds the silk cover around her naked body, and takes Semi by the hand. They exit the kitchen.

Interior: China—Villa Huang's Office in Evening

Muno and Semi enter the office hand in hand. Muno walks over to the buffet. She kneels down to look in the refrigerator under the buffet. She takes one among many bottles of precious champagne. She hands the bottle to Semi. He looks around in the room and sees the two large elephant tusks on the writing desk. He freezes and points to the tusks.

SEMI. Where do they come from?

MUNO. They have always been here.

SEMI. But why?

MUNO. I don't know. I believe Father is very proud of them. He has some kind of business with jewelries and arts.

SEMI. But—

MUNO. I don't know. Come.

Muno takes Semi by the hand. They exit the office.

Interior: China—Villa Huang's Kitchen in Evening

Muno and Semi enter the kitchen. Muno puts the champagne bottle on the table. She looks in the cabinets, finds two champagne glasses, and brings them to the table.

MUNO. Please open the bottle.

Semi opens the bottle. Champagne bubbles out of the bottle in a large stream. Muno holds her hand to the mouth and laughs. Happy but distracted, Semi fills the two glasses. Muno takes her glass and sits on Semi's lap. They touch glasses.

MUNO. Now promise me that you never leave me. Whatever happens.

SEMI. I promise.

They empty the glasses. Muno places one arm around Semi's neck and puts her head on his shoulder. He keeps her close in a magic moment. Muno fades with the champagne.

MUNO, *whispering*. Stay with me tonight. Take me up there.

Semi rises, carrying Muno. They exit.

Transition a few months forward in time.

Interior: China—Villa Huang's Kitchen in Evening

Dressed in traditional clothing, Min opens the front door. Casually dressed, Semi enters. Min greets Semi wholeheartedly.

MIN. Finally!

SEMI. I know, but it's so busy.

They walk to the low table by the windows. Min has prepared tea. She starts pouring the hot water from one pot over the tea leaves in another. She leaves the tea to steep.

MIN. Tell me everything. How are you doing?

SEMI. The examinations are coming up soon, so it's a lot of work to finish.

MIN. I am sure you are on top of it.

Min starts serving the tea. She hands Semi a cup. She pours her own cup while Semi watches her lovingly. They both hold the cups up to their lips and enjoy the soft fragrance. Min stops talking. She senses Semi has something on his mind.

MIN, *smiling.* So … what is it?

SEMI. It's about Muno.

MIN. Yes, what about her?

SEMI. She wants to be with me.

Min hesitates briefly and looks down at the table before she answers.

MIN. But Semi, that is great. She is a wonderful girl.

SEMI. Oh, yes. But what about her parents? You know how rich they are. I am sure they have great plans for her. And I … well, I am from another world. (He pauses.) And Min, I don't even know who I am.

MIN. I know, Muno. I know better than any. And I know you better than any too. (She pauses.) If that's what she says, then stay with her please. And I shall be endlessly happy for both of you.

SEMI. But the parents?

MIN. I know what you think. But I know more too. So, my boy, be happy. I know she is right for you. Be happy. Shine, my boy.

Min fills their cups with tea. They taste the strong tea. Semi appears relieved.

SEMI. Min?

MIN. Yes?

SEMI. How is it that you work for Huang's house?

Min looks down for a while before she talks.

MIN. It's a long story. I was there first. From my childhood actually. Then Jack showed up, and we got engaged. Huang helped him get a job, and he helped both of us with getting this place.

SEMI. Has Jack done the same for Huang all the time?

MIN. Yes, he always took care of these large boats. And a lot of people. (She pauses.) It's a hard job—lately even more so. Sometimes I feel something about it really bothers him. Or maybe he just got older.

SEMI. Did he ever talk about me?

MIN. Of course. He cares so much about you. And so do I.

SEMI. And when I first got here?

MIN. Well, that was a surprise, but he cared for you. You meant a lot to him, something very deep. It was good he found you—whatever happened. And you became part of me as well.

Min smiles silently. They finish the tea. They rise and walk to the exit.

MIN. Please come again soon.

Semi exits.

Exterior: China—Harbor during Day

Semi walks through the harbor, carrying his drawing papers. He sits down close to the pier where Jack's boat is usually docked. He starts drawing the scenery.

Cross Fade

Exterior: China—Harbor during Day

Jack's boat approaches the pier. Still drawing, Semi watches the boat coming to the pier. The men tighten the ropes to the pier and exit the boat. Jack appears. He's the last man to exit the boat. He carefully puts up the barrier for the entrance. He sees Semi. He hesitates for a moment and walks over to him.

JACK. Can I see?

SEMI. Sure.

Semi shows Jack several drawings of the harbor, the ships, and the people. Jack smiles.

JACK. They are good. Are they for the examination?

SEMI. Maybe some of them.

JACK. I'd better get home. Away for several months this time!

Jack walks to a car by the small administration buildings and drives away. Semi gathers his drawings. He stays for a while and watches Jack's ship carefully.

Exterior: China—Harbor in Evening

In the late evening the harbor is quiet. Semi walks down to the pier. He watches carefully to ensure he is not being watched. He reaches Jack's boat. He quickly jumps over the barrier and boards the boat.

Exterior: China—Jack's Ship at Harbor in Evening

Semi walks along the deck, looking for the entryway to the cargo room. Semi searches again using a small flashlight. Hidden behind a huge pile of fishing nets, he sees a handle to a door. He pushes the heavy nets enough to the side for him to squeeze between the nets and the metal wall to the door. The door is closed with big bolts. Semi looks around the deck. At the front of the boat, he sees a large toolbox. He finds a set of pliers and walks back to the door. He unscrews the bolts. The door opens with a squeak. Semi squeezes in and enters the cargo room.

Interior: China—Cargo Room on Jack's Ship at Harbor in Evening

Semi walks through the large cargo room, finding the way with his small flashlight. There are large bundles of fishing nets, tools, boxes, and drums. Semi walks to the back of the cargo room. Some wood captures his attention. He moves the fishing nets. A large number of large wooden boxes become visible. The boxes are firmly closed with solid nails. Semi squeezes one box open with a large metal rod. He lifts the lid enough to see the contents with his flashlight. He holds his breath when he sees multiple elephant tusks. Frightened, he steps back from the box. He sees similar boxes piled up all the way down the large cargo room. He walks farther down through the cargo room between the boxes, carrying the metal rod. Halfway down, he pries one more box open. He cries when he sees the small elephant tusks. He sinks to the floor and hides his head in his hands while he cries.

Semi hears steps on the deck. He hides. The steps get closer. A man steps down in the cargo room. A strong flashlight flickers in the room. Semi hears the trigger of a weapon, and he hides. A man approaches the boxes with open lids. The steps stop. The flashlight moves slowly through every corner of the room. It stops by Semi. The man steps in cover behind the boxes.

JACK. Come forward, or I'll shoot.

Semi comes out from his hiding spot with his hands raised. He looks into the strong flashlight, squinting his eyes. Jack lowers the flashlight. Semi tries to see the person behind the light.

JACK. You know I have to shoot you now, right?

Semi recognizes Jack's voice. He lowers his hands.

SEMI. Just do whatever your consciousness tells you—if you have any.

JACK. You remember what I told you many years ago?

SEMI. Yes, and I have held my word. But what have you done? How many murders have you committed in the meantime. Endless, I imagine.

JACK. Get out of here.

Jack waits for Semi to pass him. Then he walks behind Semi back through the cargo room and up to the deck. He secures his weapon as they reach the deck.

Exterior: China—Jack's Ship at Harbor in Evening

Semi and Jack stand face-to-face on the deck by the exit. The wind blows strongly. It rains. Semi's eyes are filled with tears.

SEMI. Why?

JACK. Please ... just go back safely.

Jack's eyes are sad. His tears blend in with the heavy rain. Desperate, Semi throws his arms around Jack's neck and holds his head on Jack's shoulder. While he is crying loudly, Jack holds his arm around Semi.

SEMI. Please, please help me ... help them. Help me. Please .... please!

They walk down to the pier.

Exterior: China—Harbor in Evening

Jack and Semi walk down the pier. Jack holds his arm around Semi. As they reach the land, Jack put his hand on Semi's head for a moment.

JACK. Please get home safely.

Semi walks away. With a worried look, Jack watched while Semi disappears in the heavy rain. A convoy of trucks appear by the pier. Jack turns and walks back to the boat. Numerous men exit the trucks and swiftly board the ship.

Exterior: China—College Lawn during Day

The students are lining up for the graduation ceremony on the lawn in the college campus. The dean is sitting on a podium surrounded by key college officials. There are numerous rows of chairs lined up on the lawn. Parent, relatives, and friends of the college watch the ceremony. Muno sits next to Min and Jack. One by one, the graduates step up on the podium. The DEAN (who's sixty and slim with gray hair) hands each student their diplomas. He congratulates them with a hearty handshake. Semi gets to the dean. He receives his diploma. Muno rises and applauds.

The last graduate student gets his diploma from the dean. The spectators, the graduates, the dean, and the college officials mingle. Muno runs to Semi and embraces him.

MUNO. Congratulations. You are wonderful.

Min and Jack follow behind. Min embraces Semi.

MIN. Congratulations, my boy. So well deserved.

Jack shakes Semi's hands and holds Semi's arm with his left hand.

JACK. Congratulations, boy.

Jack, *whispering*. Now let's build a better future.

Cross Fade

Interior: China—College Banquet Room in Evening

The banquet room is decorated for the celebration of the honorary students of the year. Invited guests, including the honorary students, their parents, and their friends, are seated at round tables. The dean, the professor of arts, and three college officials sit by a table close to the podium. Semi, Muno, Min, and Jack are at the same table. Semi is in the official graduation dress. Muno, Min, and Jack are dressed up for the celebration.

A dinner has been served. Numerous servants are clearing the tables. The dean goes to the podium. He addresses the assembly.

DEAN. This time of the year is always the most joyful for me. To congratulate all our graduates and to see their energy and devotion is indeed breathtaking. (He pauses.) And here tonight you have seen how we also acknowledge our honorary students—those who achieved the most distinguished results.

The audience applauds.

DEAN. This year our board has decided to make one more nomination for particularly distinguished results. As some of you will know, this happens rather seldom. But this year is one of those years.

The dean takes a sheet of paper from his folder.

DEAN. Let me read to you a few words from there commendation of our boards of the arts.

DEAN, *reading*. In summary, it says, the profound artistic quality of these drawings are enchanting. They bring us to a depth in our love for nature and wildlife and our future far beyond what any words will ever describe.

The dean pauses and smiles over the assembly.

DEAN. Ladies and gentlemen, these were the last words of a long recommendation and a statement of much praise. So let me now invite Semi to come to the podium and receive our appreciation and congratulations.

The dean reaches his arm toward the totally unprepared Semi. He looks around in disbelief and stands, uncertain on what to do. The entire audience starts applauding. The dean takes a few steps down toward Semi and reaches out for him. Semi takes the dean's hands and comes to the podium. The dean picks up a framed diploma and leads Semi to the center of the podium.

DEAN. My dear Semi. I don't think I need to say more. Please receive this diploma as a sign of our total appreciation, admiration, and support for your future. We know your dedication is unprecedented, and we wish you to know you have all our support as you move forward and pursue your goals and your arts. Again—and I speak on behalf of the entire college—we congratulate you.

The dean hands Semi the diploma. They shake hands and lightly embrace. The audience rises and applauds. Semi lifts the diploma and bows to the audience. He quickly walks back to his table and takes his seat. Muno smiles, full of admiration to Semi. The dean again goes to the podium.

Exterior: China—College Lawn in Evening

The delegates leave the college area through the many small paths over the lawn. Semi and Muno say goodbye to Min and Jack. They stand for a while by the entrance to the college building. As the last guests have left, they start walking down to the exit from the college area by the end of the lawn. Muno holds Semi's arm tight and lovingly.

MUNO. I am so proud of you! (She pauses.) But the best drawing is the one you made of me. And this committee has not even seen that.

They laugh as they continue to walk. A little down the path, Muno stops under a large tree. She stands opposite Semi and throws her arms around him.

MUNO. There is something else.

SEMI. Yes.

MUNO. I am pregnant!

SEMI. Are you sure?

MUNO. Yes. (She pauses.) And I am happy.

Muno moves closer to Semi and puts her head on his shoulder.

SEMI. But what do we do?

MUNO. I don't know. Stay together somewhere. You can do anything. We know that now.

SEMI. But your family?

MUNO. We'll figure something out. I don't care.

They continue the walk down to the gate. They stop a cap on the busy street. Muno steps in. She sends a loving kiss to Semi as the car drives away. Semi walks back to the college dormitory.

Interior: China—Villa Huang's Office during Day

Huang, Wei, Daiyu, and Jack are in the office. Huang reads the latest report.

HUANG. It is still not good enough. What's going on, Jack?

JACK. We have problems with the government forces. They are more widespread, and they are faster.

HUANG, *addressing Daiyu*. I thought you took care of that.

DAIYU. I did, but locally, they have geared up.

JACK. Daiyu has done a good job. But we need to know exactly what they are doing. If we know that, we can get around them. We need a mole.

HUANG. Can you organize that?

DAIYU. Sure, but I need a man we can trust.

JACK. I have that man.

Interior: China—Villa in Evening

Semi, Min, and Jack are finishing dinner at the table. Zu is taking the last plates from the table to the kitchen. The evening outside is clear, dark, silent, and fresh. Jack turns to Semi.

JACK. Let's go out in the fresh air while Min makes the tea for us.

Jack and Semi rise and go to the terrace. Zu brings the tea and bowls to the table. Min organizes the table and starts brewing the tea. In between she watches Semi and Jack through the window.

Exterior: China—Villa Terrace in Evening

Semi and Jack go to the edge of the terrace. They watch the brilliantly clear lights coming from the town.

JACK. I want to help - I want to change things. If you help me, I can do it. Will you listen?

SEMI. Of course. Tell me.

Interior: China—Villa in Evening

Semi and Jack enter and take their seats. Min has prepared the tea, and she hands them their cups. They drink in silence.

MIN. You are famous already. So what are you going to do?

SEMI. Maybe I will try to visit my country—if I can find out where it is.

MIN, *addressing Jack*. Maybe you can help?

JACK. I will.

They sit in silence.

SEMI, *addressing Min*. If I am away for some time, can you help Muno if she needs some assistance?

MIN. Of course. You know, she is so close to me.

He pauses.

MIN, *whispering*. Closer than any.

They rise. Jack and Min follow Semi to the exit. Min embraces Semi and says goodbye. Semi exits.

Exterior: China—Beach by Day

Jack is sitting on a bench by the beach. In the fresh wind, the waves are strong. A car pulls up behind him. WEINON (who's fifty) steps out of the car. He walks to the bench. Jack looks up.

JACK. Let's walk.

The two men walk down to the beach and continue along the beach. Jack hands Weinon a paper folder.

JACK. This is all the information you will need.

Jack pauses and hands Weinon an additional sheet of paper.

JACK. That's the data you need for the girl.

Weinon puts the papers inside his jacket. He hands Jack a small piece of paper.

WEINON. These are the codes you need. Learn them by heart now and throw the paper in the sea.

JACK. It will be just a couple of months. I will alert you some weeks in advance.

The two men walk back. Weinon enters his car. Jack remains sitting on the bench, watching the violent waves. He reads the numbers and walks down to the sea. He shreds the paper and throws the small pieces up in the air. They fly and spread over the sea.

Exterior: China—Jack's Ship at Harbor in Evening

Semi walks up the pier, carrying a bag with his luggage. Jack stands on the deck by the gangway. Semi boards the ship. The ship exits the harbor.

Interior: Kenya—Police Office during Day

Semi enters the small, rather primitive office of Sargent NINO (who's thirty-five). The large, extremely physically fit officer rises from his desk and greets Semi. He directs Semi to a chair in front of his desk.

NINO. Great you are here. We are impressed by the recommendation we received from the very highest level!

He smiles.

NINO. I have all your paperwork done.

He hands a file to Semi.

NINO. And most importantly, here is your ID. It gives you access to this place.

SEMI. Great. Thanks.

NINO. Let me introduce you to the team right away and show you around.

They exit the office.

Interior: Kenya—Operation Planning Office during Day

Nino and Semi enter the busy operation planning office. About ten police officers are busy with work. The room is small for the number of people. All over the place are computer screens, piles of paper, and detailed maps on the walls. The men stop working as Nino and Semi enter.

NINO. So folks, here is Semi. He will be working closely with you guys, and he will deliver crucial information for our planning.

The men welcome Semi. They are all extremely serious, focused, and marked by battle.

NINO. Your place is here. Everything should be connected and work. You enter your own password the first time you open your computer. (He pauses.) Take your time with all the folks here. And please join our planning meetings right away.

Nino exits. Semi starts activating his computer.

Interior: Kenya—Operation Planning Office in Evening

Semi, Nino, and his men are gathered by a small conference table. The OPERATION OFFICER (who's twenty-three) is standing by the maps.

NINO. Is that what we have?

OPERATION OFFICER. We are almost sure they are here now and will try to progress like this.

The operation officer points the details out on the maps.

INO. So we can hit them tomorrow. Are we still on time? OPERATION OFFICER. I believe so.

NINO. So gather a team, and we are out in ... thirty minutes.

NINO, *addressing Semi.* You should join, but stay in the background. You should only watch, but you need to see.

Exterior: Kenya—Forest at Night

A truck with heavily armed government troopers stops in the forest close by the savanna. Semi and the operation officer sit together. They all jump down from the truck. The men hide the truck in the bushes. They all walk quietly to the edge of the savanna.

OPERATION OFFICER, *addressing Semi.* You and I stay here.

OPERATION OFFICER, *addressing Muno.* Take your positions. We are in the right spot.

The men spread in the forest and hide.

Transition to Dawn

Exterior: Kenya—Forest at Dawn

A group of poachers appears at the edge of the savanna and hides behind bushes. It is silent. After a while the silence is broken by a remote trumpeting from an elephant. The poachers ready themselves for shooting. The elephants appear. A poacher rises and takes aim at the lead elephant. Muno shoots and hits the poacher in the leg. He falls to the ground, screaming. The other poachers turn around and aim their weapons toward the soldiers.

NINO, *from his hiding spot.* Throw your weapons down!

One of the poachers immediately starts shooting in Nino's direction. They return fire. The poacher is killed. Two other poachers start shootin, and they are immediately gunned down. The remaining poachers throw their weapons down and raise their hands. The soldiers move forward and arrest them.

The truck drives into the area. The bodies and the arrested soldiers are loaded on the truck. The soldiers follow. Semi looks at the dead bodies and the hurt poachers. The truck drives away.

Exterior: China—Villa Huang's Gate at Night

Five police cars pull up in front of the gate. Heavily armed policemen exit the car. The security guards appear, and they are immediately told to throw their weapons down and open the gate. The police cars quickly drive to the front door of the mansion.

Exterior: China—Villa Huang's Main Door at Night

Policemen quickly unlock the door. A police officer and several other men enter the building. Shortly after that, the officer appears, pushing Huang and Daiyu in front of him. Numerous policemen enter the building. Huang and Daiyu are pushed into a police car, and they are driven to the station. Policemen carry computers and piles of paper out of the building and load everything into the cars. The building is sealed. The cars leave. A few men are left to guard the house.

Interior: China—Hospital at Night

Muno is in labor in an operation room. A doctor, a midwife, and two nurses assist her. Muno screams in pain as her baby is delivered. Smiling, the MIDWIFE (who's forty) carries the child to a small table, cleans it, and wraps it. She hands the newborn baby to Muno.

MIDWIFE. It's a boy, dear. Everything is fine. As healthy as healthy can be!

Muno takes the baby and holds it firmly close to her body.

Exterior: Kenya—Landing Strip in Evening

Jack is with thirty gunmen by a primitive hide for helicopters. Three helicopters are parks between the men. Three small planes are parked by the runway.

JACK. Folks, we are up to the biggest catch ever. All the herds will get together tomorrow morning. We move in with three teams. And we take everything. (He pauses.) There will be big rewards for all of you.

GUNMAN 1. Are we sure the ground is clear?

JACK. Absolutely. Our folks on the ground know what's going on. (He pauses.) Any questions? Okay, folks. Get some sleep.

Exterior: Kenya—Forest in Evening

A column of five trucks stop at the edge of the savanna. Semi, Nino, and about fifty heavily armed men get off the trucks. Nino directs the men. They all hide around the lake by the edge of the forest.

Cross Fade

Exterior: Kenya—Forest at Dawn

The men on the ground are hiding and anxiously watching the horizon and the lake. They can hear the trumpeting of elephants in the distance. The men watch several herds approaching the lake. The herds with multiple baby elephants and their mothers start drinking and bathing in the water. A huge lead elephant watches from the edge of the lake.

Suddenly, the large elephanthears the distant sound of helicopters approaching. The men on the ground prepare their weapons. With incredible noise, three helicopters approach the heard. The men open the doors in the helicopters. The gunmen point their weapons as they maneuver into position. The helicopters fly low toward the herds withdrawing from the lake.

Nino gives everyone the sign. His men open fire at the helicopters. They are all hit by grenades. The helicopters make emergency landings. The gunmen run out of the burning helicopters and start shooting at the men on the ground.

The soldiers open fire on the gunmen again. Most of the gunmen fall dead to the ground. The fire ceases. The remaining gunmen throw their weapons down and raise their arms. Jack comes from the helicopter with his arms raised.

Semi, Nino, and their men approach the surrendering men in order to arrest them. Semi's men quickly disarm the gunmen. When Jack sees Semi, he smiles. His gunman notices.

GUNMAN 1, *shouting.* You traitor! You set us up.

Semi sees the gunman draw a pistol from his pocket and take aim at Jack. Semi runs to him to prevent the shooting.

SEMI. Don't!

Semi throws himself between the gunman and Jack. He is hit by a bullet from the pistol. He falls to the ground, bleeding heavily. His men immediately shoot the gunman. He falls to the ground. Jack kneels down to Semi. As Semi senses Jack, he whispers. Unable to hear, Jack moves his head close to Semi while the men try to halt the bleeding.

SEMI, *whispering.* Just tell Muno that I wanted to stay. Don't say anything else. Please.

Semi closes his eyes. Soaked in his blood, Jack cries, his head on Semi's chest. A group of people from the village hear all the noise and start walking toward the men. As they get closer, Luno, who recognized Semi from the distance, runs ahead of the group. She falls on her knees next to him. Still conscious, Semi recognizes her. He takes her hand. She bends over him, crying desperately.

The huge lead elephant approaches the group. The men all recoil, frightened, and they pull the prisoners with them. Semi and Luno are alone as the elephant walks toward them. Luno looks up and stands when she sees the elephant approaching. She stands up, Semi bleeding by her feet. She does not move as the elephant gets closer and closer.

The elephant stops within centimeters of Luno. It trumpets a sad sound when it recognizes Semi. It takes its trunk down to the still conscious Semi. It touches his hand slightly. Semi opens his eyes and looks up at the large elephant. He looks at the leg of the elephant and sees the wound. He smiles weakly, and with his hand, he touches the elephant's trunk and holds it. He closes his eyes as he dies, his hand still on the elephant's trunk.

The elephant makes a weak, mourning sound. With Luno still standing next to Semi's body, the elephant lifts the body and carries it to the edge of the forest. A group of the other elephants follow. Under a large tree, the elephant places the body in a small hollow in the ground. It starts taking branches from the trees in the area to cover the body. The other elephants follow, and they all cover Semi's body with branches. When the body is totally covered, the elephants gather around it and mourn. A small baby elephant puts the last small branch with flowers on the mound. The elephants stay around the body while the men gather the prisoners and put the bodies on the trucks. When they are ready to leave, Jack and Muno watch the scene.

NINO. We will have to take him with us.

JACK. No, he stays here.

As they enter the truck, they see Luno on her knees by Semi's grave, surrounded be the elephants. The trucks drive away.

Interior: China—Villa during Day

There's a knock on the front door. Min opens the door. Muno is standing outside, carrying her baby.

MIN. My dear, what happened?

MUNO. The house is closed. There are nobody there. Only guards. I cannot get in. Can I stay here?

MIN. Of course. Come in, dear.

Min steps aside. Muno enters. She shows Min the child. They both smile.

Transition Months ahead

Exterior: China—Harbor at Dawn

Min and Muno are in the harbor where the pier reaches the land. Muno is carrying her baby and looks toward the entry to the harbor. The fishing trawler appears and approaches the pier. Muno runs out on the pier and stands by the landing site. She sees Jack on the deck. The boat is tied to the pier, and the gangway is put in place. Muno looks anxiously for Semi. Jack walks down the gangway. Muno runs up to him as he reaches the pier.

MUNO. Where is Semi?

JACK. He stayed. He asked me to tell you something.

Muno holds the baby tight and cries.

MUNO. It cannot be. He wants to see his child. It cannot be. What happened?

Jack gets tears in his eyes as he looks at Muno and the child.

JACK. That's what he told me to tell you. There's nothing I could do.

MIN. I don't believe this.

Min runs out on the pier to Muno and sits down by her.

Interior: China—Villa in Evening

Jack, Muno, and Min are sitting by the table. Min serves the tea. Muno is holding her baby. There's a knock on the door. Min and Muno look surprised. Jack goes to the front door and opens it. Weinon is outside. His driver and car are in the background. Jack asks him to come in. Min and Muno rise.

WEINON. Muno?

MUNO. Yes.

WEINON. I have to tell you that your parents have been tried today.

MUNO. Yes?

WEINON. And for now they will remain in jail. And by the way, so will Mr. Wei.

MUNO. But why?

WEINON. I cannot tell you, but I have some papers for you.

MUNO. Papers? Why?

WEINON. They give you access to the house. You can pick up your personal things. Otherwise, the house is sealed, and you will have no access. Later, when the case is over, the house will be yours.

Weinon hands Muno a few papers. Jack watched very attentively.

WEINON. You just show these papers to the guards to get in.

Weinon takes out a small folder with additional papers.

WEINON. And here are some additional papers. They give you access to bank accounts that were set up in your name. They are not affected by the case. So you are a wealthy woman.

Weinon hands the folder to Muno and says goodbye. Jack follows him to the front door. He comes back to Muno and Min, who are both still standing.

MIN. What is going on? You must know.

Jack shakes his head and leaves to room.

Interior: China—Press Room in Government Building in Evening

The press room is packed with journalists, officials, and invited guests. Weinon is seated in the front row with high-ranking officials in uniform. Min sits among the invited guests. The side door opens. The MINSTER OF JUSTICE (who's forty- nine) enters with Jack and two officials. He takes the stand and speaks to the assembly.

MINISTER OF JUSTICE. I am pleased to be with you all here today. I have great news and an important announcement. (He pauses.) As you know, we recently unveiled and disrupted one of the largest groups ever engaged in the illegal trafficking of endangered species, which was in violation of all international treaties. In addition, we have unveiled an enormous chain of tax fraud, money laundering, and bribery.

The minister of justice turns toward Jack.

MINISTER OF JUSTICE. I'd like today to honor Jack Zang as the driving force behind these successful accomplishments. Because of what Jack did, we have been recognized, and we have received appreciation from our partners across the world.

The minister of justice and all in the room applaud.

MINISTER OF JUSTICE. And let me now make an announcement. In our continued efforts to fight the lawless pursuit of the wildlife in the world and to eliminate all the associated unlawfulness across the world, we have established a new department focused entirely on these tasks. And I am glad and proud to announce that Jack Zang will lead this department. He will report directly to me. He will be fully empowered in the pursuit of our goal to totally eliminate the dangers to the wildlife across the world. We have informed our international partners of these important steps, and we have aligned our efforts with those abroad. Given the recent events, I am sure you will agree that we could not possibly find a more suited leader of this now immensely funded and important effort. And I would like to not only congratulate Jack but also thank him for undertaking this task.

He turns to Jack, shakes his hand, and embraces him while the applauding audience rises.

Interior: China—Villa in Evening

Min and Jack are by the table, both avoiding eye contact in a tense atmosphere.

MIN, *extremely tense*. I am your wife. You have to tell me the truth.

JACK. When I tell you that I am now doing everything good in spite of terrible mistakes in the past, then I am telling you the truth. The tide has turned.

MIN. And Semi? JACK. I told you.

Muno enters, carrying her child. She sits down and looks at Jack and Min.

MUNO, *whispering.* Where is he?

JACK. I told you what he said.

They sit in silence for a while.

MUNO. Please take me to the place you last saw him.

Muno and Min both look down in silence.

Cross Fade

Exterior: Kenya—Forest at Dawn

A soldier drives a small open jeep through the forest. Muno is holding her child, sitting in the back seat next to a heavily armed soldier. Jack, who's unarmed, sits next to the driver. They reach the area in front of the village. Jack and Muno walk to the small gate and enter the village.

Exterior: Kenya—Village at Dawn

The families are making fires in small groups across the village and preparing their breakfast. Luno sits by one of the families and prepares the food. As Jack and Muno enter the gate, the families stop their preparations and sit unmoved. A man from the nearest group rises and walks to Jack and Muno. They stand face-to-face for quite a while.

JACK, *in Swahili.* Luno? Semi's mother?

The man looks around among the families. He spots Luno and points at her. Jack directs Muno to follow him. They reach Luno. She rises and stands firm, straight, and proud. They stand face-to-face for a while. Jack greets Luno.

JACK, *in Swahili.* I am Jack. This is Muno ... and your grandson.

Luno moves close to Muno and watches the child. Muno hands her the child. Luno takes the child and holds it close.

LUNO. It is like Semi. It is his child!

Luno steps away from Jack and Muno and walks slowly all around in the village, holding the child close. She turns around and around to show the child the village and the forest. Luno stops in the middle of the village and watches the gate.

Cross Fade—Flashback

Exterior: Kenya—Village at Dawn

Semi (who's six) is leaving the gate, holding Ramo in his hand. They disappear in the forest while they heard the trumpeting of elephants in the distance.

Cross Fade back to Present

Exterior: Kenya—Village at Dawn

Luno carries the child and then goes back to Jack and Muno. She hands the child back to Muno.

MUNO. Ask her where Semi is please. JACK, *addressing Luno.* She asks about Semi.

Luno signals Muno to follow her. They walk together to the gate. Jack remains in the village, following them with his eyes.

Exterior: Kenya—Forest at Dawn

Luno and Muno walk along the forest at the edge of the savanna. The huge red sun rises over the terrific landscape. They reach the open area by the lake. They walk to the large tree. Where the elephants buried Semi, there is a large group of flowers. Luno kneels down by the flowers and hides her face in her hands. With the child, Muno stands close behind her. Tears pour from her eyes. The huge elephant appears and approaches them. Frightened, Muno thinks about running. Luno stands and holds Muno tight. They stand close, their arms behind each other's backs. The elephant comes close. Luno holds the still frightened Muno tight. As the elephant moves closer, Muno feels Luno's tranquility. The two women stand side by side with the child. The elephant stops centimeters from them. It lifts its trunk to Luno. She touches it gently. It moves its trunk to Muno. She touches it gently without hesitation. Finally, the elephant touches the child gently and makes a soft sound. The huge elephant turns around and slowly walks away. Luno and Muno stand side by side and follow the elephant with their eyes.

The picture fades. A text documenting the statistics of elephant killings and the associated human sufferings play on the screen.

www.ingramcontent.com/pod-product-compliance
Lightning Source LLC
Chambersburg PA
CBHW070451170726
48291CB00005B/1704
* 9 7 8 1 9 4 9 7 4 6 8 3 9 *